D1458187

THE ECSTASY OF ANGUS

Books by Liam O'Flaherty
from Wolfhound Press

The Pedlar's Revenge and Other Stories (1976)
Skerrett (1977)
All Things Come of Age: A Rabbit Story (1977)
The Test of Courage (1977)
The Wilderness (1978)

If ever there was an art on which the whole community of mankind has worked — seasoned with the philosophy of the codger on the warf and singing with the music of the spheres — it is this of the ageless tale.

Joseph Campbell's Introduction to Grimm's *Collected Tales*.

Liam O'Flaherty

THE ECSTASY OF ANGUS

Illustrated by Lucy Kilroy

WOLFHOUND PRESS

©1978 Liam O'Flaherty
Afterword ©1978 A. A. Kelly
Illustrations ©WolfhoundPress
ISBN 0 905473 18 3

Published 1978
Wolfhound Press
98 Ardilaun
Portmarnock,.County Dublin.

The Ecstasy of Angus was originally published
in a limited edition, London 1931.

Published with the assistance of the Arts Council.

The Ecstasy of Angus

THE ECSTASY OF ANGUS

FOR many years the ever-youthful Angus, god of love, had wandered through the land, saving his mortal children from dark Crom, the demon lord of death. Everywhere his golden beauty triumphed. Maidens, on seeing him, grew tender with desire and then conceived of mortal swains in hope that concentration on the image of the god's sweet countenance would counteract the alien instruments that forced their wombs.

Young men, envious of his perfect form, brought wives into their beds, so that children might issue from their seed and rival Angus. And thus Banba was peopled. When weary parents, emptied of their fruit, departed to the fairyland of Youth, their children continued to obey the urging of the golden god. Just as, when a stone cast into a silent pool, the water's rim is curled in an eddy that circles, recurring, to the shores and each ring begets another greater than itself, so each generation multiplied, until every glen and mountain-side and grassy plain was peopled.

And he also ministered to the needs of man's vassals, the beasts, the birds, the insects, the fishes and everything that breeds increase by union.

On hearing his seductive voice, wild stallions grew rampant in the heathered glens and set upon their slender-fetlocked mares the furious impress of their towering satin tubes, whose luscious sap re-issued from the wombs as giddy foals, to fill the plains with prancing herds. So also did the wolves and boars increase, the sheep, the goats, the hunting dogs, the kine and all the four-foot beasts that leap upon their mates. The singing birds received his special care. They circled like living garlands round his head, when he went his way, blessing the feasts of love. They grew so numerous that the volume of their music rose into the farthest corners of the air and made smooth the turbulent winds. He kissed the flowers that gave their sweetness to the honey bees and they, returning to their hives with golden loot upon their daggers, fed unto their queen the god's love potion, so that she rose in spring attended by her drones and mated in the air and filled the cells with fertile eggs. He looked into the waters of the brooks beneath the willow boughs where the she trout had spawned and with the fire of his glance made the spawn glitter, so that the he trout, passing, grew enamoured of their beauty and kissed them with his supple belly. And so with the insects too, they answered to the tender spurring of his feet and multiplied.

He filled all the green island of Banba with living things and the fleshless hands of Crom were empty.

Then the crowded land offered no further room for generation. The innocent joy of begetting grew corrupt, finding no outlet, and death began his conquest of young lives, who slew one another in the fury of their baffled love. Joining together in their tribes, they fought their rivals for woods and grassy plains and fish-bearing rivers. So that famine and desolation followed and the soul of Angus grew over-vast with lonely doubt, not knowing what answer he should give to the wailing prayers of his people.

Then he journeyed to the west, to Arranmore, beneath whose towering cliffs, in magic caves, the great god Mananaan held court for the ocean sprites, mermaids and fishes that inhabit the seven seas.

THE palace of Mananaan lay within a dark-blue bay, surrounded on three sides by sheer cliffs, whose faces were cut in tiers by mighty caverns. The fairy hosts inhabited the caverns in the upper cliffs. The god's dwelling-place lay within, through a circular door cut in the centre of the arc, above the water-line. The door was curtained by a thick veil of ever-falling purple brine. It was guarded by a troop of savage seals, whose terrible tusks and endless moaning drove off all trespassers. A road of sea-foam led from the door to a flat, square rock of great dimension which lay out in the bay, its sides adorned with hanging red and yellow weeds, which swayed as the murmuring waves rose and fell with the labour of their tides. Upon this rock, the god was resting on a couch of perfumed sea moss, having his evening bath. Little green sprites sponged his limbs and combed his raven beard. Others tickled his spine, his loins and the soles of his feet with tiny brushes made of seals' fur. Mermaids wound their sinuous, snow-white bodies back and forth through his arms. A giant conger eel encircled his neck and kissed his ears with its silken snout. Before him on a tangled mat of shinning weeds, a troupe of she fairies danced in a row, holding a curtain of transparent sea-grass before 'hem, so that their half-concealed, voluptuous leaping became magically coloured by the red rays of the sun. Overhead there was a circling flock of eagles, hawks, and gannets, and other tribes of birds floated on the waters of the bay. There also, a host of fishes swam, come to do homage to Mananaan, mammoth whales joyously spouting fountains of brine, sharks cutting the waves with their knife-like fins, porpoises turning somersaults, salmon leaping high and kissing their tails, eels forming labyrinthine figures with their twisting bodies, rockfish showing their jewelled bellies.

From out the teeming sea, an overpowering perfume rose into the nostrils of the god, so that he laughed mightily and stretched his limbs, rejoicing in the greatness of his strength and in the wisdom which enabled him to fashion and procure his subtle pleasures.

Angus, watching from the cliff-top, frowned, comparing his own wretchedness with Mananaan's secure happiness. Then he called a flock of doves and breathed a message into their beaks and they, soaring into the air, glided down to Mananaan and passing before him, dropped into his ears the words of Angus in the order of their utterance.

"Mananaan, most wise and ancient of the gods, Angus, son of Youth, has come to you with the burden of his sorrow, for he is weary of the task imposed on him. Your encircling sea impedes the outspread of the mortal men and women born in my likeness. They are most dear to me of all the living things that owe their life and increase to the wine of love that is distilled into their veins from my immortal being. Here in this land that is the fairest ornament swimming in your seven seas I have created beings resembling in their beauty the immortal gods, and they have increased to such a multitude at my bidding that not a single nook is ignorant of their laughter, which banishes the rough winds and robs the cloudy chaos of its gloom. My life force must flow outwards in a never-ending stream, and as streams flow to the sea, so must my land encroach upon your ocean, dry up the fringes of its bed and make green with juicy grasses and with fruitful trees the churlish, barren sands."

On hearing these words, Mananaan sent for a school of flying fish which came towards him, rising on the foam-capped crest of a mighty wave. The wave stood still with arched head until the god had spoken his message. Then it shot forward towards the cliff and the flying fish rose, flapping their silver wings, to the cliff top and dropped their words at the feet of Angus, as they circled on their downward flight.

"Angus, your words are as the stinging hail with which the hostile powers of chaos lash my ocean's back. Such anger is the outcome of your rash conceit, which drove you to the senseless task of making mortal beings in your own image, but without the fulness of your power. Restless, passionate youth, with little knowledge you undertook a monstrous labour, which required wisdom beyond the comprehension of your feverish mind. It is beyond my power to help you in the manner you require; for the ocean is untamed and if I tamper with the shuttle of its tides, dam its mouth or give to you the smooth strands on which my young fish are nourished, then the waves shall rise in furious rebellion. Before the avalanche of their advancing breakers the whole land shall crumble and be plunged into the ocean's bowels. And thus shall perish the offspring of your foolish love, devoured by monstrous, blubber-headed fish."

Angus answered him bitterly:

"Ungrateful Mananaan! Perversion of all godly sentiments! Have your unseemly habits so corrupted your immortal memory that you forget I am the author of the countless lives that sport within the waters of your seas? When you make merry riding on a dolphin's back or lech with the voluptuous eels, or take joy in the leaping of the salmon or the gambols of the mighty whales, do you forget that it was through my loving agency your arid, moaning desert became fruitful? Base and libidinous glutton! Your seas remain untamed and its inhabitants continually at war, mutually devouring, for your rule is barren of purpose, being contained within the narrow circuit of satisfying your lusts."

Then Mananaan was taken by a frenzied anger, and

leaping to his feet, he strode about the rock, crying aloud in his thunderous voice:

"Arise, arise, lords of the four winds, unloose your savage hurricanes and pelt upon my ocean's back cataracts of hail from the frozen poles. Rouse my foaming chargers and send them thundering on the shores of this land of Banba. Up, waves, from your deepest caverns, advance and spit your lashing brine upon the face of this insulting god. Overflow this land, root out its trees, tear up its soil, up-turn its mountains, crush every living thing you find thereon and sweep the rubble to the deepest ocean pit."

Then he mounted on a dolphin's back and rode into his palace, through the curtain of ever-falling purple brine, attended by his sprites, his eel, his mermaids and his concubines. The fishes dived into the sea and fled, some out into the depths, others hiding in clefts of rocks from the fury of the oncoming storm. The fairy hosts descended from their caverns and followed the god into his palace. The guardian seals retired within the curtain and lay there in a flapping mass, moaning. The birds rose into the air, cackling loudly and soared above the land, waiting for plunder. The sky grew black. The sun's rim sank into the ocean. From the sky came a monstrous roar, the signal for the storm, reverberating with increasing force to all the corners of the world, where the winds stood waiting.

Then the winds rushed forth and fell upon the sagging bellies of the clouds, which broke from their moorings and were carried at headlong speed, tossed like gigantic balls by the conflicting gusts. Clashing with their mates, their bladders burst, their skins caught fire, which flew in deadly streams downwards to the land and crashing on tall trees brought them screaming and uprooted to the ground. The belching water was frozen into balls by the icy winds. Some fell upon the waves, like whips, to incite the ocean's anger. Others swarmed on the land, killing the young buds and grasses. Up rose the waves, careering, whipped by their furious jockeys, who tore off the soothing oily wrap lain on the ocean's back by the warm sun, dug their sharp spurs into the purple waters and drove them to the shores in towering ranks, foaming at their jaws. From all sides they came in wild confusion and clashing in their furious onset, sent columns of glittering brine high into the air, as far as the drifting tendrils of the torn clouds. The tumult rocked the ocean to its deepest bowels and from unspeakable dark caverns, monstrous fishes, rocks and hairy weeds rolled to the surface and were carried on the breakers to the land. The waves climbed up the cliffs, striking great blows that shook the earth and the insatiable winds, carrying loads of brine and foam upon their wings, swept inland, blasting all growth, overturning trees, destroying beasts, men, birds and insects.

The Ecstasy of Angus

NGUS fled from the cliff, pursued by the particular fury of the hostile elements that bore allegiance to Mananaan. With him fled the burrowing animals that lived there, rabbits, weasels and mice, together with the little singing birds and the flock of doves that always attended him. Hot in pursuit came the thunder, lightning and the winds, laden with brine and hail, ravaging all growth that could not flee, the pretty, perfumed hillside flowers and the tender plants that grow in crevices, so tenderly beautiful that even the kindly sun dare not kiss them with the fulness of his rays. All was swept naked from the rocks, where savage cormorants and gulls roamed feasting on the slain. Dark night had now encompassed all the land, except when the lightning flashes made lurid the rainswept rocks and the hills, down which flowed swollen streams.

Then Angus took shelter in a glen beneath an overhanging ledge of rock. A little stream flowed from the rock's face, through ivy and ferns. Nourishing the soil of the glen, it made green and flowering all the roots and seeds. Beds of sweet-scented flowers, ferns, cresses and wild clover grew among the grass, and beneath the ledge there were dry and warm beds where deer were wont to rest. A delicious peace filled the place, more sweet because of the tumult that raged above it. The god lay down exhausted, bleeding and torn by the hail and by the rocks on which he had fallen in his flight.

As he lay there, the animals and birds surrounded him in order to protect him from the storm with their furry bodies. They licked his wounds and soothed him with their melodious voices. Cheered and comforted by such love, he fell asleep.

Then the fury of the storm spent itself. The winds returned to the four quarters whence they had come. The sea fell. The moon arose and the sky grew radiant with the heavenly lamps that guide the fairies of the night.

THEN Angus stirred in his sleep, feeling a warm breath upon his face. Awaking, he heard a voice whisper his name. He shuddered with delight at the caressing sound. No bird had ever warbled music of such sweetness. The warmest summer wind, blowing at midday through the heather on a mountain slope, did not carry such passionate desire upon its breath. His blood coursed in fever through his veins, heated by the exciting presence of the speaker. He opened his eyes and saw a woman of extraordinary beauty bending over him. He cried in ecstasy:

"What fairy loveliness is this that conquers the combined glories of the sun and moon? Are you reality or do I dream, halfwitted and create the opposite of the barbarian beings I saw wantoning about the slothful body of Mananaan? Unspeakable grandeur, perhaps you are no dream but in reality some fairy princess come to banish the dark weariness I suffer at the malicious hands of my enemies. Here I lie trembling like a salmon that has overleapt a fall on to a river bank and flogs the damp, green grass with frenzied tail. My eyes are scaled with the dried tears of sorrow. I cannot see your features with sufficient skill to know if your eyes shine on me in friendship or in enmity. Tell me your name and the purpose of your visit to Angus, the star of whose greatness has fallen so low that, even the surly hurricanes of chaos are free to buffet him."

The woman stood erect and opened wide the cloak that hung loose about her body. Then she said:

"Look, Angus, look upon me shining within the beauty of my magic cloak. Then your eyes shall lose the scaly mists of fear. Your trembling limbs shall then regain their supple leaping power and in the joy born of my loveliness you shall forget your woes. I come to you neither in hate nor friendship but in love. I am the fairy princess, Fand."

Her magic cloak was colourless without, so that she was invisible when fully enveloped in its folds. Its marvels were within, facing her body, which was devoid of other covering. The whole of Banba had been ransacked by cunning wood sprites and river nymphs to procure the gems and precious stuffs that fashioned it. Hundreds of revolving rays danced upon her snow-white skin, making the heavenly beauty of her body absorb by reflection the glory of each precious thing that shone upon it.

Contrasting colours, interwoven, drew dusky scarves across her rounded busts and over the well which lay where the alabaster pillars of her thighs joined in a triangle of curling roots, illumined her raven hair, gilded her flashing teeth and filled the mysterious pools of her eyes with divine images. The air around grew sweet with perfume and the earth stirred gently, as when at dawn in spring the budding seeds do shudder in their shells beneath the lustful kisses of the sun.

She stood still while Angus gazed in adoring wonder. Seeing that his countenance grew dark and that he trembled violently, she whispered:

"Does not my beauty please you, Angus? Am I less fair than those mortal women on whom you smile? Do you suspect me ignorant of love's art, unworthy to enfold in the embraces of your tower-like body, or think that I entice you to a vain pursuit, meaning to cheat your passion of its victory?"

She stroked his golden hair. He shuddered and said in a faint voice:

"Would that it were so! You surpass in beauty the loveliest mortal woman that I have created, as a sunbeam surpasses its own dark shadow. But I am vowed to chastity and must remain innocent of love's delights, lest I spread knowledge of sin among my people. The blind fury of Mananaan's host was nothing compared to the torture of desire I now suffer. I am a thirsting toper and you a flask of wine held beyond my reach."

The fairy woman laughed. Her laughter re-echoed through the glen and then was carried on either side across the land by hosts of pretty fairies, who caught the wandering sounds and made the blood of Angus tingle with desire. Then Fand drew her cloak about her and became invisible. Angus stretched out his hands in despair.

"Do not fear, Angus," she said softly. "I am still with you, but I have concealed the beauty of my body in order that you may appreciate the wisdom of my mind, without being disturbed by the noisy turmoil of your hungry blood. You have gone to Mananaan and he has refused you help, but I am going to deliver you and your mortal children from the encircling net in which you are enmeshed, by teaching you my art, which you in turn shall impart to men and women. For a long, long time I've been enslaved by your beauty and have used many a charm to stay the fury of your feet, that you might draw aside by moonlight in some lonely dell and lay your tired golden head upon my bosom. But like a wild colt that flies before the summer's turgid heat, passes over the plain like a whirlwind and plunges headlong into the foaming sea to cool the excess of his heat, so your flying feet were deaf to my calling, as is the colt to the wistful whinnies of his budding mare. But now the surly waves have thrown your dripping body torn to the shore. My love shall be the balm to heal your wounds and give fresh impulse to the gay career of your creative soil. On the winds of my love you shall soar higher than the topmost stars in the firmament. Thy love and mine combined in tender unison shall rob the most alien corners of the universe of their dark secrets. The golden tower of your strength shall have no summit, when you begin to build with the assistance of my cunning hands.''

Then Angus answered her and said:

''Alas! Sweet queen, my father Youth has warned me that I must pay the penalty of eternal chastity for the favour of being allowed to create men and women in my likeness. Should I trangress, even with you who are the loveliest of beings, the produce of my love shall be visited by dreadful punishments. Thenceforth licentious lust shall follow in my tracks. My face shall bear the impress of my infidelity to my sworn vow and poison the minds of all who look upon it. Women shall turn from the pleasures of their marriage beds to find promiscuous satisfaction of their lusts. They shall eschew the wise division of their sex, bar the seed of life from entering their wombs by shrewd devices and make merry with all manner of lewd vice among their kind, lest the lordly phallus should distort their bellies and their breasts in the toils of motherhood. So too shall men become corrupt and slay, with their own hands, the unborn children of their loins. Drugs and wine shall make them sots, without the power to raise love's wand in homage, when their hearts crave for prattling images of their infancy. A horde of whores and skinny woman-loving jades and painted boys

24

shall spread disease by their foul practices. Even corpses rotting in their tombs shall be defiled and mongrel monstrosities shall issue from fearful matings. War and famine shall come as curses on this profligacy. Death shall jeer at me, as he passes with his laden truck of breathless beings. All manner of unclean and poisonous germs shall multiply, begotten of the sin I would commit by tasting the honey of your love.''

Again she opened her cloak, and bending over him, encircled him within its folds, so that his head lay against her bosom. And she whispered:

"Here between the snowy mounds of my breasts, soft, swooning love shall overcome the memory of that foolish vow, which the jealous ignorance of your father Youth imposed on you, lest Angus, grown to Manhood through the food of wisdom, should reach a magnificence beyond the comprehension of the gods themselves. Sleep, sweet love, while I bear you to my magic tent. There you shall awaken to find my promises do not do justice to the ecstasy you shall experience.''

The Ecstasy of Angus

T HEN she vanished into the air, invisible within her cloak, with Angus asleep upon her bosom, accompanied by her fairies. They passed in a cloud of mist, high above the earth, at a great speed, until they came to a valley which lay among high mountains. There the cloud flew along the course of a river that wound through a thick pine wood, upward towards its source and settled in a green glade by the river bank. Fand opened her cloak and cried:

"Come, all my merry little men and women, welcome Angus to my couch. Surround this grassy carpet with a silken roof. Bring from the mountain caves your pretty instruments and make music for my love. Bring jewels to deck his body and perfumes to anoint him. Mix him a liquor from the strongest juices to inflame his blood and set his thoughts careering. Weave garlands of wild flowers for his hair. Come, dancers, to guide the movements of his limbs in imitation of your magic leapings, and singers, let you pour into his ears poetic whispers which shall re-issue from his lips as battle cries during the culmination of our tender onsets. This night my heart is spendthrift and I lay all the store of my charms upon the bosom of Angus, the golden god of love."

Angus, awakened from his swoon and seeing Fand in all the beauty of her nakedness before him, became possessed by such a passionate love for her that he forgot his vow and his sorrow. He arose, stretched out his arms exultingly and cried:

"No more shall I feel proud of my innocence. Rather shall I consider myself forever accursed and like a lascivious monk eunuch doomed to sly brooding on lost happiness unless I ravish you this instant."

With that he tried to embrace her, but she stepped aside and said:

"Our love shall be ceremonious, a sacred rite, with due regard for the dignity of each emotion, and not a savage orgy, unfit for your divine character. Look round. Admire the beauties of this place and thus become gradually attuned to the magic properties of the love which you are going to taste. For by this love you shall be re-born, with a power hitherto unknown among the gods. And so you must approach my love with fitting reverence. Look round while I command my singers to commence."

Angus grew calm and did as she bid him.

The Ecstasy of Angus

ON every side tall mountains rose to the horizons of the starry sky. Their lower slopes were covered with trees, heather and various flowering shrubs, whose wild odours gave strength to the air, so that it seemed like floating wine. Higher up, the slopes were bare but no less beautiful, for there the naked earth assumed strange shapes and seemed to sway with roundness, as the heights and hollows interlaced, climbing on rocky terraces to the peaks that touched the clouds. Then, growing blue and dim in the distance, they looked like giants with pointed heads, standing guard above the valley. Down the centre of the glen the river flowed, jumping through rock gorges with a great prattle, lit by the moonlight, which made bright its fountains and covered its dark winding pools with strange shadows. There fishes leaped in chase after the hordes of flies that buzzed upon the water and water birds were flopping by the banks, or scurrying with a great flutter of dripping wings through the shallows, courting their mates. Like a dappled snake the river flowed, while the trees bent over it, as if enamoured of its beauty or its voice, whose tingling melodies re-echoed through the mountain caverns. In this gentle tournament of rival beauties the pine trees were in no way conscious of defeat, for they stood proudly erect, with their many arms extended wide, like strong men stretching their muscles; and their fan-like branches, sucking the dew, spread an awning over the earth where their horny roots entwined and the grass was

pale from hunger, robbed of its sap. But fairest of all
was the green, grassy field, between the rim of the pine
wood and the river bank. Here were little flowers
growing in profusion among the grass, whose gentle
blades gave hospitality to the sweetest buds that come
from nature's womb. As the wine-strong perfume of
the pines made the air drunken with passion, so the
meek scents of the flowers softened its fury with
caresses.

Angus was so much exalted by the magic beauty of
the place that he bowed down and made reverence to
the earth, saying:

"Banba, to-night I bless you in thanksgiving for the
joy your moonlit beauty has given me, and I now
command that all my children born on your lap shall
love and reverence your beauty in equal measure to my
love, so that even the most boorish heart shall be
stirred to softness by the glamour of your green mantle
and by the mystic shadows on your hills."

Then Fand spread her cloak upon the grass and
made him sit with her upon it. She took his hand and
said:

"Beloved! Tell me if you still fear to disobey the
promise that your father exacted from you? Do you
desire me with a singing heart or does some furtive
demon thought make mischief in your mind and

disarrange the whirling power of your passion? If so our courtship would result in barren remorse, If not sing to me of your love."

She looked into his eyes and his eyes grew moist with love. As he opened his lips to speak, a score of tiny fairy maidens issued from the pines, naked but for a shining gem that each wore in her navel. They joined hands and began to sing, while the pine branches swayed in accompaniment, making a faint mysterious music with their clashing needles. Their words entered his ears and then issued from his lips in praise of her, assaulting the fortress of her passion with their fire.

As he spoke he was possessed by the first state of ecstasy, the whirlwinds of words:

"Terrible queen, my only fear is that you might vanish from my sight or become indifferent to my love before my body's juices reach your womb and close its doors upon my generating image. You are terrible like the blazing sun, before whose brightness every eye must fall in adoration; but as the sun's warmth gives life and strength to every growing thing, so does the warmth of your beauty cause my life's bud to rush springing from its shell and point its daring head at the portals of your love. You are the source of all merriment and beauty. No more can I feel exalted by the lark's rhapsody or by the warbling of blackbirds at sunset, for your voice shall sing for ever in my ears and silence coarser melodies. Having seen your naked body I shall find snow dark, a young foal heavy of limb, a fountain clumsy in its shape and the rose but a poor image of your fragrant lips. As you have unified all beauty in your being I must remain your begging slave for ever, furious and passionate when the recurring madness of my love urges me to steal that unity by union and then waiting till another madness helps me to renew my hopeless theft."

As he finished speaking he reached out to encircle her with his arms, but she drew back, laughed and jumped to her feet. She ran dancing over the grass and unloosed her hair until it floated round her head like a black wheel with countless spokes as she whirled on her toes. She stretched out her arms and made them ripple from the shoulders to the wrists, and then, ceasing to whirl, she began to make eel-like movements with her trunk. The little fairies ran to her and clutched her falling hair and deftly wove it into plaits which they entwined about her throat, her shoulders and her breasts, so that she seemed embraced, dancing, by a score of snakes. Then, sinking down as in a swoon, she writhed on the grass and her attendants began to caress her with their tongues. She gradually grew still. Then they left her, formed a single rank and began to dance towards Angus, with outstretched tongues, which mimed the leaping of flames. They curved and thrust and slid upon the air, as when above a roaring forest fire the heavy smoke is full of winding, leaping tongues, that lick the hidden heads of trees with their consuming fervour.

And as they came near, Angus, distraught with passion, tore off his clothes and then laid himself naked for their administrations, while he gazed at Fand, who returned his glances, both of them exalted by the ecstasy of dancing tongues.

Then the fairies fell upon him in a polite frenzy, touching each most tender and responsive nerve and sinew with their rosy daggers, whose bloodless wounds, inflicted on his pores, sent their sweet agonies shooting through the fabric of his being, so that each muscle grew wild with delicious longing and buckled up its utmost strength in gorgeous pride, which did inspire his mind with reckless lavishness. Into the countless streams of his tingling blood, his tissues shed their substance. He cried out, unable to endure their pricking kisses. And Fand, watching him, stretched out her arms, when she saw that he was charged with love to overflowing. But when he rose to come to her, casting the fairies roughly from his body, she uttered a loud cry, and mocking terror, covered her bosom with her palms.

Immediately the glade grew full of sound, as all her sprites and nymphs rushed to protect her, from the river and the wood and the mountain caves. Some were shaped like birds, others like flies, while some were shaped like women, with swollen bellies and long winding cords hanging from their navels. And as Angus rushed upon her, the birds flew into his face screaming, the insects stung him and the women pulled their cords and swinging them about their heads, lassoed him in his flight.

A blind fury seized him and he clawed at his assailants, striving to ward off their lacerating blows, but the lashing cords encompassed his limbs and he was impotent. So he bowed his head, exhausted and suffered them to lash him as they willed, and immediately submission changed the pain of laceration into ecstasy.

The Ecstasy of Angus

HIS blood cooled. The onrush of his seed
was stayed. He sank to the ground, closed
his eyes, stretched out his limbs and
sighed. Then Fand ordered her minions to
desist. They vanished. She lay beside him and
whispered:

"Beloved, do you love me still? Or has this
chastisement frozen the budding flower of your
passion? Let not your heart convulse with jealous
anger, because I test with stinging blows, delay and
feigned displeasure the courage of its will to love. It is
no perverse whim that makes me toy with your
approaches, but in order that your final victory may be
richer with the spoils of hard-fought battles: that each
fibre of your being, at the moment of your triumph,
may feel it earned its reward. You cannot take me like a
wolf, which gorges on its bloody prey ere the heart has
ceased to throb, but like a subtle god, who with most
delicate senses contemplates the many beauties of the
feast, before the first morsel touches his palate. Sweet
love, be merry and dispand those furrows on your
brow and tell me that your tenderness is still at fever
point."

He seized her fiercely by the wrist and looked at her
with glittering anger in his eyes. His baulked strength
grew rigid with shame that such a delicate being could
regulate its uses. And he said:

"Just as the guardian thorns of the rose do wound the hand that plucks their flower, so have your servants wounded me and through the wounds inflicted by their blows a demon entered. My love for you still lives but hatred is mounted on its back and does corrupt my blood that rushes to embrace you. So that I want to crush you in my strength. So have I seen wild beasts tussle in their matings and in the frenzy of her lust the tigress gashes with her claws from root to tip the unprotected member of her mate. The beastly temper of the tigress lies concealed behind the divine beauty of your body. The brute fury with which you have infected me is the curse of my infidelity already destroying my godly innocence. But as a tiger has claws and fangs stronger than his mate, so shall I wreak my vengeance, now that I hold you in my grasp. Your loveliness and my desire shall be no safeguard against my destroying fury, which shall drink the precious blood that gushes from your torn flanks and from your mangled breasts."

But when he seized her with both hands to do violence to her body, he became limp and held her in a soft embrace, while she lay unresisting in his arms, her whole body melting with tender love, that moistened her eyes, her lips, the paps of her breasts and the mouth of the channel to her womb.

"My golden lord," she whispered, "a tiger does not gash his mate when she lies wanton in his paws, as I lie now against your comely belly which, like a silken sail hollowed by the wind, flutters with the panting of your heart. My love, talk not now of tigers and of torrid lust but of sweet birds that twitter beak to beak which kisses make them preen the downy plumage of their breasts and close their beady eyes in ecstasy. Now let our exultant souls go soaring wing to wing and contemplate the tender sweetness of all gentle things.''

With limbs enlaced and breast to breast they lay in an ecstasy of tenderness.

THEN Angus whispered:
"No more shall I compare you to a tigress, but to a lily, whose shapely stalk and dazzling bloom charms the rude and soulless earth, so that it makes a valley in its lap to shelter the sweet flower from the barbarous wind. As I look into your eyes the mirrors of my soul reflect and make manifest all the images of beauty that have enthralled me wandering in this land and made me long for some unknown, unfathomable happiness, of which their beauty was a sign. So did I sigh with longing when the

sighing breezes in a tree-filled valley played upon the clustering leaves and the tapering trunks did sway in mystic rhythm and a withered twig, dislodged, came falling from the topmost branch; the whispering solitude did echo in my bosom and cause pain, whose source I could not fathom. It was my lonely heart that swelled with longing for your love.

"All joy and beauty made me restless and unsatisfied and mournful, like a lost sheep when parted from its flock upon a foggy moor, with downcast head it bleats into the smoking vapours that have concealed the light and turned the earth into a dun wilderness, full of damp and dreadful fantasies, rotting smells and gloomy silence. At times I heard with terror the distant plaintive cry of a fowl, when the sun had just begun its downward course and the parched earth lay still and weary, after the triumphant, singing tumult of the dewy morn; stark cries of timid birds, foreboding doom and dissolution. And so with shining beauties that seemed perfect, without stain, complete in rich, full-bodied harmony, like leaping fountains, or flowers in their bloom, or swallows on the wing, all were possessed of some dark force that made me shudder, even while joy in their beauty made my breath halt in my throat.

"But now, beloved, the world is rid of longing and of all dark, fearful emotions. While I hold you in my arms, my strength scoffs at sorrow, as the giant oak, with roots deep-embedded in the earth, scoffs at the storms that lash his shining trunk."

Then she took his face within her palms and kissed his lips. Their eyes closed and they lay in a swoon, with their lips joined, with limp limbs, shivering in ecstasy. With their lips parted, his head sank to her bosom, and looking at him with wondering eyes, she whispered:

"Oh! Loveliness! Why has the wine of your breath upon my tongue made me so drunk with misty foolishness that the store of my speech is powerless to give me words worthy of your beauty? For my burning heart must burst or find relief in pouring fiery songs into your ears. Would that I had the swift power of the west wind to carry you in my embrace high into the heavens, held within my grasp so tightly that even the smallest hairs of your body could feel my kisses. You are so lovely that I am now overwhelmed with remorse because I dared allow my servants to offend you. I crave pardon with my kisses."

She kissed him from head to foot and then had her maids bring perfume, with which she anointed him so that all blemishes were removed from those parts which had been lashed or stung. And as she rubbed with cunning hands, his courage, which had lain like the limp stalk of a wet flower, rose stiff like a great pine, whose bark cracks, unable to contain its mighty strength. She spoke as she anointed him:

"Now raise my tent, my merry architects, midway between the pine wood and the brook, upon that dark green place round which a circular wreath of daffodils is growing. Within its silken dome prepare my couch, that I may caress my love. Bring from your store rooms dry reeds, steeped in the sap of young pine trees. Lay them for flooring to my tent. Gather abundance of wild flowers and lay them on the reeds. Let my musicians stand ready with their instruments and my cup-bearer come with a love-draught. Bring all my veils and ornaments that I may add to the desire of my beloved by cunning artifice."

FROM all sides a host of fairies appeared in the glade and got busy fulfilling her commands. The little hunch-backed masons gathered round the circle of daffodils, and pulling strands of silk from their humps, began to weave the dome, in many colours, so deftly woven that on the curving wall a multitude of pictures appeared, of a description suited to the purposes of love. The moonlight pierced the half-transparent wall and lit the interior with most pleasant and seductive brilliance. Other little men brought bundles of reeds with which they wove a mat. Still others came laden with flowers, which they cast in confusion upon the reeds, until there was sufficient for a bed. And so the tent was made ready.

Then the musicians appeared with their instruments and stood ready waiting for the signal of their mistress. There were pipers, harpists, lute-players, buglers and a host of others with mysterious instruments, suggestive by their shapes of potent love-making.

But most wonderful was the treasure borne by the fairy maidens that came to dress their princess. They moved like a whispering wind with the rustling of the veils they carried, and their jewels were almost terrible because of the many dazzling lights that poured from them. They decked her in her veils and ornaments and put a bridal crown upon her head. They dressed him

also in a long robe and crowned his head and placed a
sceptre in his hand.

Then the cup-bearer came with his bowl. He was a
bearded little man, with a wrinkled face and laughing
eyes, of enormous paunch and with a bush that quite
concealed his crutch, spreading like a pair of
moustaches to the angles of his loins and hanging
down his thighs in plaits. His chest was adorned with
a pair of teats, shaped like the stoppers of wine flasks.
The summit of his crown was bald, with a curly rim of
hair, in which flowers, ferns, and moss were entwined.

First Angus drank, then Fand, then Angus, and so
until the bowl was emptied and the bowl-bearer
returned to his store to refill his measure.

Then Fand took Angus by the hand to lead him to
the tent. And both of them felt fire ascending to their
minds and an ecstasy of drunkenness unlocked the
doors of their imaginations, which came forth dancing, and released bubbling thoughts from their wine-
red gloves, being conceptions of lewd follies.

The Ecstasy of Angus

NOW from the mountains came the sound of drums, beating in harmony, which began low and distant, like a throbbing in the bosom of the earth, when the internal fires are bubbling at the rim of their rocky casing and with their force bore channels to the surface land, which rises in a mountainous boil and from its ulcered mouth pours lava down its slopes. This angry hum grew suddenly more loud, quickened its pace and stirred the currents of the air with its commotion, so that the trees swayed, the mountains trembled and the river water foamed about its banks in curling, golden eddies.

As they walked to the tent, two maidens followed, bearing the magic cloak of Fand, which they carried so that its inner radiance lit the loving pair and warmed them with a voluptuous heat. And when they reached the door and the drumming was at its height, the other musicians joined the music of their instruments to the wild tumult. Now it seemed that all the harmonies of nature had been caged by music and then let forth, with all the coarseness of their substance drained, set in such order that their varied sounds were joined in melody and yet retained the glorious sweetness or wild, romantic power of their origin, so that there was unrolled through this majestic symphony before the listening mind of Angus a panorama of the world's beauties, hurled in confusion by squandering ecstasy.

The Ecstasy of Angus

There they saw great rivers pour from snowy mountains, swollen with a flood of snow and ice, which, melted by the sun, came in an avalanche and burst the river banks, bearing trees, rocks and clammy soil into the surly torrent, so that it rushed into the plain and spread afar like a sea on which a horrid mass of debris sailed, drowned men and animals, houses and the inner painted layers of the earth colouring its swirling tides. Simultaneous with this exuberant destruction, which was the central vein of the symphony, more delicate themes created, in quivering, soft tones, images of nature's gentleness, the summer's dewy dawn, upon a plain, where sunlight is shining on the grass and a herd of horses are galloping with swinging tails, or the sunset with its singing birds and lovely shadows, its distant sleepy cries, its mists that trail like fairy veils across the purple mountains. There, too, was autumn with moaning winds that bear the dead leaves to their coffins in the earth and sombre winter with his snows, his silence and his smoking breath. Then came rampant spring, who, rising from his lair among the winter's snow, stretches his frosty limbs and with cool, soft rain and sunny heat softens the calloused earth, so that it sprouts with springing buds that fiercely thrust their heads into the air's stinging energy. So was all beauty balanced in this tournament of sound and made perfect by comparison with ugliness, that black concubine, whose sullied loins make beauty's love more sweet.

The Ecstasy of Angus

They entered the tent and the two attendant maids hung the magic cloak upon the doorway, so that its jewels, shining on the flowery bed, made it warm like a shallow pool in a rock by the sea's edge, where yellow moss is growing, steeped in brine, and the hot sun plays upon it and the shore birds walk on long red legs back and forth through the salty shining moss, cackling with delight. Now the music sank into a whisper like a cry of yearning heard in the night from a wild bird that has flown far out into the high air above the ocean, seeking a lost mate. Then again, when they lay down among the flowers, their souls hushed into a swooning timidness by the plaintive whispering, the music filled its belly with a savage power.

Then Angus, startled from his swoon by the furious, low-sounding, bursting blast of music, saw a black stream swimming in a cloudy place, of such dim form that the water seemed to fly on air and the transparent shores laid bare its full proportions, which rushed without descending on an endless course, like an eel, swift, and like a bird, singing in its flight, and like the wind, stinging, and like the risen sea, all-conquering, merciless. And the ecstasy of power entered unto him.

H E bared his body and then, seizing Fand, he bared her also, uttering cries of joy as his hands tore her precious veils and roughly pulled the golden bangles from her wrists and touched her loins, her swelling breasts and her white throat, until all was naked and white and smooth like swandown, and she lay panting, with closed eyes, indifferent, already drugged by the approach of his lust, which had now sucked all his strength, and with taut spear pointed made ready to carry by assault her willing love. Then he sprang upon her, rigid like a hawk which swoops from the sky, a golden arrow flashing in the sun, upon a furry chick. She answered with the bounding motion of a hare at play in a field of young corn.

They babbled, sang, laughed, kissed and shouted as their bodies moved, dancing with increasing speed, and like a pair of dancers miming battle, now they paused, quite still, watching. Then he made a sudden thrust, they embraced, cried out and swayed, stretching. Then he feigned retreat and she in mock terror pursued and drew him back until he stood again encamped before her womb and she held him gripped.

Then suddenly they both grew incoherent and shook with a palsy that was like the dance of death, but that it was more fierce, joyous, and exuberant and exuded heat instead of clammy cold.

A great cloud of incense rose from the flowers on which they lay, enshrouded Angus, quivering on her breast, and with its touch upon each gaping pore of his toiling body, forced his multitudinous seed into her womb. He shuddered, groaned, and then lay still, dazed, limp, empty. Then he closed his eyes, slid from her and slept. The music ceased. Then all was still as in a tomb or in a sandy desert where the parched earth is never moistened by the rain or dew, but lies always still, an idle wilderness, beneath the gaping sun.

Such was the ensuing stillness in the tent.

Then Fand moved. At first she raised her head and looked at Angus. Her eyes had become subtle, cunning, lit by the cold gleam with which the eyes of a preying bird watch a dying animal, which it fears to kill, but waits until death's cold grip has crushed the struggling heart. Then she smiled faintly and drew aside into a corner of the tent, where she sat musing, breathing gently, fondling her belly with her hands. Slowly her expression changed; she looked upon her sleeping lover until her eyes dilated and her forehead knit and her lips curled with tense passion. Then, as if distraught, she whispered:

"Lo! I have conceived of him. I hold his seed entombed within my womb."

She stroked her belly, musing. She looked at him again and said:

The Ecstasy of Angus

"He lies like a dead pine tree or like a golden eagle, fallen from the clouds, with helpless wings outstretched; and any little timid bird may peck at those closed eyes that were once so terrible in their beauty. See how his slack belly twitches and his fair skin hangs like a windless sail about his heaving lungs. He ran upon the plains as swift as a young colt, but now his winged feet are limp. His legs are as the stalks of trampled flowers. His veins are pale, for I have sucked the redness of his blood, which swells within me. Oh! Joy! Most royal theft, that stole the seed of kings from a god's loins and left a sleeping carcass for the crows to pick."

Then her voice grew tender and she whispered, with bowed head, rocking gently, holding her arms clasped on her bosom like a mother rocking a babe:

"Safe in the locked casket of my womb this little bud shall grow into a darling image of my love. My warm blood shall feed its growth until I feel its tiny feet move within me and my swelling body shall bear proud witness to the giant it breeds. I shall fill these twin breasts with sweet milk for the time of his forthcoming. And he shall suckle at my paps and sleep upon my bosom with my limp teat dangling in his rosy lips. I shall listen in rapture to each breath of my little one. I shall cover him in rich garments and play with him upon the grass, when he begins to crow and laugh and chase the stars in my eyes with his chubby

48

thumbs. Oh! My joy is sweet as honey and there is a wild song in my heart because of this great power which has come to me. A power without end, for this seed shall beget seed, all royal, godly seed, and I shall be the mother of a host of kings."

Then she rose silently, took her magic cloak from the doorway, wrapped it round her and left the tent. Still Angus slept. While the approaching dawn began to drive the cloudy cinctures from the mountain peaks with its sharp breath, the virtuous forerunner of the sun, it drove off all the sinful fantasies of night and made the earth fresh and comely for the embraces of the lord of light. The inhabitants of darkness vanished, bringing with them all the unnatural accoutrements of their magic revelries. When the first rays of the risen sun streamed down the gleaming sides of the mountains into the glade, Angus lay, without a covering, on a heap of trampled flowers and reeds, naked.

FEELING the sun's warmth, he stretched himself, opened his eyes, and sat up. He saw a strange sight that made him shudder and brought the pain of impending doom into his heart. And he became aware that he had become transformed in the night, losing his youth, his beauty and his strength. His limbs were stiff. The flesh had fallen from his bones. His skin was wrinkled and withered like a leaf in autumn. His face was furrowed and unknown to his hands, as they touched his harsh cheeks in horrid wonder.

Before him in the glade he saw a great tree which had miraculously risen in the night. Its branches were covered with sweet-smelling blossom, which came falling to the ground in showers, as if wafted by a soft breeze, although the air was still and the blossoms in falling did not diminish the volume of the tree's blooming. Delicious music issued from the trunk and a host of birds soared about its summit. The whole tree quivered, from root to topmost branch, with the whirring motion of a bat which, sleeping on a warm rock, is disturbed by some internal passion and, taken by a frenzy, unfolds its wings and dances in its sleep, beating the air with such speed that its whole body seems to whirl and there is a buzzing sound. Yet the bat sleeps and does not move. So did this tree quiver in orgastic movement.

A gloomy spirit stood near by, clothed in shining

The Ecstasy of Angus

armour from head to foot, with one hand holding a great shield over his heart, while with the other he grasped a spear. His face struck terror into Angus. Passions unknown among the gods, or among the mortal beings he had created with his breath, were imaged in this spirit's eyes. And yet, although the eyes looked evil and terrifying, they were fascinating, like the eyes of a snake before it leaps and shoots the venom of its tongue. They held the glorious melancholy of incurable unhappiness, the lust of conquest and the pride of genius.

Angus struggled to his feet, unseemly with the bedraggled flowers and torn reeds that stuck to his head, in the tangle of his loins and on his wrinkled rump; an old man, trembling, ribbed like a hungry horse.

He cried out to the spirit:

"Who are you and whence comes this tree, whose properties are alien from those of any tree grown by my will? Are you a god, and if so by what authority have you come into this land where none but I may live?"

The spirit answered:

"I am the Genius of Unrest and this the Tree of Knowledge. I am neither god nor human, since I am part of universal space, of which neither gods nor humans have yet gained comprehension. And I am here on this earth by virtue of your impotence, to finish what you have begun."

Then Angus cried out in rage:

"Surly spirit, how dare you strut before me armed with these strange weapons and insult me with mad words, taking advantage of the spell cast upon me by her who was just now my concubine? Where is she? Are you another of her tricking sprites?"

Calmly the spirit answered him:

"She sits beneath that tree. Behold the shining crown upon its trunk, shaped like a new moon, bristling with shafts of fire, which is the ecstasy of genius that descends upon the babe she bears within her womb."

H E pointed to the tree, but although Angus stared he saw nothing on the trunk and saw no one sitting at the roots. And he cried out in a faint voice:

"Woe to me, who have become the sinful victim of a demon's lust and for my sin have lost, in one short night, the uses of my eyes, so that a deadly pox has spread the rash of blindness over their spheres. I see nothing but a dancing tree and your mad figure. Everything is somersault. I am old, drugged, helpless. My father's curse is on me. What babe is this you prate about? Did you put ice into my blood, or does some wicked enemy hold a sieve between me and the sun, so that the heat is skimmed from its rays and I shiver in the cold light that filters through?"

The spirit raised his spear and threatened Angus with it. Then he spoke with great vehemence:

"Your fury shall avail you nothing, so be still, since you admit it was through your own act that you encompassed your destruction and that of all your fellows, the company of gods. They are all dead."

Angus uttered a shriek of horror and covered his face. The spirit continued calmly:

"They are all dead. You are no longer god but an old man, weak and near your death. All gods cease to be when your seed entered Fand's womb and came to life. She shall bring forth a godless son, born in your image but of the earth's substance. And his seed shall conquer the universe through the dual agency of this tree's knowledge and my genius. I shall enter unto him at birth and impregnate his mind with my quality, which shall give him no peace, until the cycle of his life has been completed and he hands on his task to his successors."

Angus sank to the ground, and clutching at the blades of grass, he tore them from their roots and moaned:

"Sweet shoots, that made a silken road for my swift feet and a warm pillow for my head at noon, how dare you still be young and fresh when Angus has grown old? They heed me not. My breath, which gave them life, is now a bitter dew upon their backs. I crawl among them like a snail, leaving a rimy trail from slavering lips, and not one blade bows its head in homage."

Then the spirit approached and said:

"Have courage, Angus. By your death you shall gain a greater immortality and a greater power than you possessed among the gods, who were but the barbarous predecessors of human genius; for your love shall be the noblest and most precious spirit in man and you shall live through that and be adored with every breath that man shall breathe. And through your progeny you shall attain lordship over all the universe. Your son shall teach his children such art as shall enable them to harness the earth's forces to their use and climb the skies on wings, so that the whirling stars of the firmament shall fall beneath their sway. Unto the end of time they shall pursue a repetition of your love's ecstasy. So do not mourn for your withered shell, when your young seed is safe embedded in good soil."

But Angus moaned:

"What is the universe to me, compared to one lock of the golden plumage I have lost? What are the whirling stars compared to my own eyes, that have lost their lustre? What is this bastard son, who has sprung from the corruption of my lust and is come to life a parricide, imbued with savage passions, a black-browed miscreant, whose sacrilegious hands are doomed to ravish every holy secret of the earth and firmament? I curse him ere the horror of this infamy force out the dregs of life from my strangled soul. And I place him under spell to remain for ever the victim of her who has dethroned me from the godly throne of youth and innocence; so that she shall for ever inspire him with the same maddening lust and shall in the same way for ever rob him of his strength, his youth and his wisdom, and cheat him for a few short moments with delicious ecstasy, only to make the ensuing despair more death-giving. Let her be a foil to his genius and let my curse go with her and her daughters. With my last breath I curse this land of Banba, which shall henceforth be poisoned to its deepest layer, so that continual war shall desecrate its beauty. With my last breath I curse the children of Banba, unless they rise and slay this son of mine, who has denied and slain his father. Lo! The sky grows dark and the godless sea does roar in mourning for the death of Mananaan, and from all the corners of the firmament the ungoverned winds unloose their fury. The earth shakes. I die. My breath is waning. I curse, I curse with my last breath, man, whose blood shall be salt and who shall for ever languish in desolate pain."

THEN Angus died amid a tumult of all the elements, and the cry of a new-born babe came from the tree and the spirit struck his spear upon his shield and cried:

"Hail! Genius is born."

AFTERWORD
by
A. A. Kelly

This tale, so imaginative and exuberant, is a fine example of the storyteller's art, but it also contains the kernel of O'Flaherty's artistic philosophy. It reveals the contradictory influences behind his work, his attitude towards man, nature, violence and the evils inherent in modern society.

In writing his creation myth O'Flaherty draws upon Irish legend but alters it to suit his purpose. Banba, his green and fertile isle, first land to emerge from the waters, was in Irish tradition the first woman to settle in Ireland before the primaeval flood — an earth-mother archetype. She stood for life in opposition to Crom, the demon lord of death.

Aengus Mac Og was the ancient Irish god of youth and beauty. In O'Flaherty's myth he holds sway over an idyllic kingdom similar to the earthly paradise of Tir na nOg (land of the young), to which the Tuatha de Danaan supposedly retreated after they had been conquered by the Milesians.

The Ecstasy of Angus

Apart from Irish legend another influence for O'Flaherty was William Larminie's long heroic poems *Fand and Moytura* (1892). "Fand" tells how Cuchulain, famed hero of the *Ulster Cycle* legends, is enticed by the goddess Fand. Emer, Cuchulain's wife, warns him that as a human if he becomes Fand's lover he will die. In Irish legend Fand is sister to Aengus and wife to Mananaan. O'Flaherty changes the situation by making a god Angus mate with an earth-fairy Fand, fairies in Irish tradition being fallen angels.

The heretical biblical implications of O'Flaherty's myth resulted in a 1931 edition limited to three hundred and sixty-five signed copies. According to the Bible Adam was created in God's image and only fell when he ate the forbidden fruit from the tree of knowledge. Like Adam, Angus falls through a female and has foreknowledge of what will ensue from his disobedience. Divine love and earthly lust, *agape* and *eros*, will mingle for perpetuity in his progeny, offspring of the ideal and the physical. O'Flaherty has moved the origin of the Fall back to man's conception. O'Flaherty's first man is born victim of an inescapable duality for which he himself is not responsible. By doing this O'Flaherty abolishes the doctrine of Original Sin, to expiate which Christians believe Christ was crucified.

In the book of Genesis God gives Adam dominion over nature, but O'Flaherty's first man is part of nature, as changeable as nature and as subject to the elements. Angus, like Adam, falls through disobedience against the father-figure's edict. The nature of the sin is not — as in the Garden of Eden — to acquire forbidden knowledge, but to prostitute divine love to lust.

The fairy Fand, who is not one of Angus's created beings on Banba, emerges as dominant, not subject to or emanating from the male as Eve did. Male and female are thus polarised. Male/female mutual dependency follows, with potential for both cooperation and antagonism.

These four differences between the Genesis creation myth and O'Flaherty's creation myth, the origin of the sinful act, the nature of the act itself, Adam's place in nature and the autonomous female figure, are all important for the interpretation of O'Flaherty's subsequent work.

The reader might well ask what indeed would have happened in the Garden of Eden had Adam and Eve been faced with a population explosion? Is chastity really a godlike attribute? These are more than whimsical questions. The myth ironically reflects the ancient superstition that too much sexual intercourse is weakening, mingled with the subsequent Christian encouragement of chastity as a superior state, and the association of extra-marital sex with sin. It also contains allegoric consistency in that Banba (earth), Angus (spirit or air), Mananaan (water) and the Genius of Unrest (fire), represents the four elements.

The over-spill problem on Banba is answered indirectly by Angus when he curses and condemns future generations to continual warfare. This is a depressing conclusion, but man has one redeeming quality. He is not raised above nature by his capacity for thought, but by the spiritual love inherited from his godlike father which 'shall be the noblest and most precious spirit in man'.

The ecstasy of Angus is therefore a state of rapture, trance and frenzy — all at once. O'Flaherty has first soared with Milton's 'seraph wings of ecstasy' and then in Hamlet's words 'blasted with ecstasy' the hopes of his protagonist.